SNOWY

VALENTINE

Written & Illustrated

by Starlene O'Neal

Snowy Valentine

written

&

illustrated

by

Starlene O'Neal

First Edition

2019

This book is dedicated to
my daughter
Samantha

I opened my eyes and looked around my room.
Lyndsey, my baby sister was waking up too.

I smiled at her. She grinned back at me.

"Happy Valentines Day Lyndsey", I said as I stretched and
got out of my bed.

"It's going to be a fun day"!

I ran to the kitchen and POPPED around the corner!

I say, "Happy Valentines Day Mom and Dad"!

They both said, "Happy Valentines Day Samantha"!

Oh! That's me!

I'm Samantha!

After breakfast I run to get ready for school.

I think my red shirt with a heart on it and my purple pants look good.

I then brush my teeth and comb my hair.
I find my blue and white long hat, blue gloves and my book bag.

"Mom! I'm ready", I yell! "Get your scarf and your boots on too sweetie! It's snowing outside", says Mom.

Dad is ready for work, and Mom has Lyndsey all bundled up for the ride to my school, and to the babysitter.

I ask, "Are we all ready"?

I then open the door and out into the snow we go!

We all wave bye to Dad as he drives off to the Air Force Base to work.

As Mom is buckling Lyndsey into the car seat ~ I'm trying to catch some of the BIG fluffy snowflakes in my mouth!

I'm getting a little dizzy from twirling around trying to catch the snowflakes.

Oh! I see an envelope in the snowy grass next to mom. It looks old. It has a really neat heart on the back!

"Mom you dropped this", I say as I hand the yellowed, old looking envelope to her.

Before driving away my Mom said,
"Hmmm, I wonder where this came from," as she picked the envelope up off the seat.

"It has a cool heart on it", I say.   "Yes," said Mom. "That's a wax seal." "It's unbroken, so its never been opened."

Mom flipped the envelope over.   "It says, 'To My Love, Millie', " Mom read from the front of it. "Millie is our neighbor! We will bring this to her tonight," Mom said putting it down.

With hugs and waves good-bye from Lyndsey and Mom,

I go out into the wonderful snow!

I skipped across the bridge to the playground and wait with
all the other kids for the bell to ring.

I'm in the First Grade this year! Miss Ista is my teacher.
Everyone thinks she is a really good teacher. She's fun too!

We start the morning with our role call to see who is here
and who is not. Then we say The Pledge of Allegiance to
the Flag.

FLAG

We've been learning it in sign language too! Neat, huh?

Once we all get settled in and are quiet. Miss Ista has us all go to the 'Square Area' in our room.

This is where the calendar and our 'Weather Bear' is.

We live in South Dakota.
Today is February 14th, (Valentines Day), it is snowing and blowing and is very cold!

On the way to the Cafeteria for lunch time ~ I see my best friend Dejtia!

Dejtia lives next door to us.
She is in Kindergarten this year.

We wave and say, "Happy Valentines Day" at the same time!

After lunch, we normally go outside for recess. But with the snow today, we are having 'free-time' in our classrooms.

Everyone is talking about the Valentines' Party we are going to have later!

Katie, Jason and I start chanting,

"PARTY! PARTY! PARTY!"

Everyone joins in!

Miss Ista then clapped her hands and shut off the lights.

We all became quiet.

"Okay, free-time is over, back to work", says Miss Ista.

We work on some Math problems on the board, and then Miss Ista has us color in our learning packets.

While we are coloring my Mom comes in with the ice-cream!

"Yay"! Everyone is getting excited!

"Okay, class," Miss Ista says, "I think we are almost ready for our Valentines Party"! "If you could please clean up your math papers and learning packets and put them all away into your desks, you can then come over here to the Square area and sit quietly."

Everyone quickly puts their pencils and papers away, and runs (quietly), to a spot on the carpet in the Square area!

It's Party Time!

We are ready!

My Mom and Miss Ista have all the ice-cream scooped into yellow cups.

We get to choose from all kinds of items to put onto our ice-cream. There are crushed cookies, nuts, colorful sprinkles and gummy worms! There is chocolate, strawberry, and caramel sauces AND whipped cream too!

Of course, Miss Ista and my Mom help us.
Or we would have had a HUGE mess!

After we all finished our ice-cream sundaes, we got to hand out and open our Valentines from every person in the classroom! Miss Ista gave us each a candy necklace with a Valentine on it!

Everyone is talking excitedly and laughing!

That was a fun party!
We all help to clean up the room and put everything back where it belongs.

Miss Ista gives us all hugs as we leave school for the day.
Homeward bound ~ in the snow!

After dinner I help my Mom with the dishes.

I ask, "Mom, are we going to bring that envelope to Ms. Millie"?

"Oh yes," Mom said. "We should bring that over there right now."

"Hello Ms. Millie. I think I found something of yours this morning in the snow. It kind of looks old and it has your name on it", I said to Ms. Millie when she opened the door.

"Well hello ladies", Ms. Millie said. "Come-in, Come-in from the snow!" "I'll make us some hot cocoa and we will take a look at this envelope you found".

"Wow, Ms. Millie", I exclaimed!" "These paintings are so pretty"! "Did you paint them"? I ask.

"No sweetie, my husband Harris painted those. He sure did love color in his works", Ms. Millie said with a wistful smile.

"Fifteen years ago Harris was out in the back woods with his paints, and I never saw him again. Nothing was found in the investigation. That painting with the tree, up top there, was the only thing left."

Ms. Millie shook herself. "Well the hot-cocoa should be ready. Lets go sit down and see this envelope."

Ms. Millie, Mom and I all sat down at a pretty table in the kitchen. "MMM-mmm-MMM, Miss Millie, this cocoa smells so delicious", I said happily!

Ms. Millie looked over and smiled, "I use real chocolate in it," she said with a grin.

"Now let me see this envelope of yours".

I handed the envelope to her.

"OH my! This looks like my husband Harris's writing," Ms.
Millie exclaimed! "It does look old too," she said while
looking curiously at it. She flipped the envelope over and
broke that red heart wax seal. Ms. Millie then pulled out a
heart shaped card!

Her eyes scanned the card fast inside and out! She flipped it over, looked at the back, then opened it again! Ms. Millie's eyes filled up with tears.

"This card is from my Harris"! "He made it too"!
She read what was written on the inside out loud to my Mom and I.

"It says;

'My Dear Millie, Look at my paintings and know that I'm near by ~ Come See! Open the door! Love Always, Your Harris' ."

"What could he ever have meant by those words"?, asked my Mom. "I don't know," answered Ms. Millie. "I wonder when this was written too," Ms. Millie said still looking at the Valentine in disbelief.

"Oh my dear Samantha," Ms. Millie looked at her with tear-filled eyes, "this is the **BEST Valentines Day Ever**"!   And she hugged Samantha so tight!

"Thank you! Thank you! Thank you!"

As Samantha snuggled into her warm covers and hugged her pillow tight, she thought, "Wow, what a great day it was! Everyone was laughing and happy today! I love it when everyone feels loved, happy and special"!

I am going to try and make **every day** be like Valentines Day from now on"!

... and she fell asleep with a huge smile on her face.

Good-night.

Dear Reader,   8/2019

I hope you enjoyed this book as much as I have enjoyed creating it!

I originally wrote, (well scratched out an idea), for this book in 1994, after coming home from volunteering at my daughter Samantha's school Valentines Party.

Here it is, 25 years later in book form!

This is my 2nd book in print.

First one is "The World of Amelia".

Lots of my books will have 'tie-in's' to 'The World of Amelia'. (Like this one did) ~(did you catch it)?

Watch for the clues in the illustrations.

Use your imagination and explore the wonders of another world!

Thank you,

Star

Feel free to find me,

FB Group: **The World of Amelia**~ I post sneak-peeks, and photos of myself and my drawings there. You can share your photos/and or thoughts regarding 'The World of Amelia' here too! I would love to hear from you!

My Books are sold on Amazon.com ~ search Starlene O'Neal

Etsy.com: my store name is: **StarZArtCorner**

InstaGram: star_oneal

59747109R00019